Parents and Caregivers,

Here are a few ways to support your beginning reader:

- Talk with your child about the ideas addressed in the story.
- Discuss each illustration, mentioning the characters, where they are, and what they are doing.
- Read with expression, pointing to each word.
- Talk about why the character did what he or she did and what your child would do in that situation.
- Help your child connect with characters and events in the story.

Remember, reading with your child should be fun, not forced.

Gail Saunders-Smith, Ph.D

Padres y personas que cuidan niños,

Aquí encontrarán algunas formas de apoyar al lector que recién se inicia:

- Hable con su niño/a sobre las ideas desarrolladas en el cuento.
- Discuta cada ilustración, mencionando los personajes, dónde se encuentran y qué están haciendo.
- Lea con expresión, señalando cada palabra.
- Hable sobre por qué el personaje hizo lo que hizo y qué haría su niño/a en esa situación.
- Ayude al niño/a a conectarse con los personajes y los eventos del cuento.

Recuerde, leer con su hijo/a debe ser algo divertido, no forzado.

Gail Saunders-Smith, Ph.D

BILINGUAL STONE ARCH **READERS**

are published by Stone Arch Books, a Capstone imprint
1710 Roe Crest Drive, North Mankato, Minnesota 56003.
www.capstonepub.com

Library of Congress Cataloging-in-Publication data is available on the
Library of Congress website.

ISBN: 978-1-4342-3778-1 (hardcover)
ISBN: 978-1-4342-3917-4 (paperback)

Art Director: Bob Lentz
Graphic Designer: Hilary Wacholz
Original Translation: Claudia Heck
Translation Services: Strictly Spanish
Reading Consultants: Gail Saunders-Smith, Ph.D; Melinda Melton Crow, M.Ed;
Laurie K. Holland, Media Specialist

Printed in the United States of America in Stevens Point, Wisconsin.
102011   006404WZS12

TRUCOS EN LA PATINETA
SKATE TRICK

Un cuento sobre Robot y Rico

A Robot and Rico Story

por/by Anastasia Suen
ilustrado por /illustrated by Mike Laughead

STONE ARCH BOOKS
a capstone imprint

This is ROBOT. Robot has lots of tools. He uses the tools to help his best friend, Rico.

Este es ROBOT. Robot tiene muchas herramientas. Él usa las herramientas para ayudar a su mejor amigo, Rico.

Teapot/
Tetera

Wings/
Alas

Scissors/
Tijeras

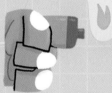

Fire Finger/
Dedo de fuego

Special Shoes/
Zapatos especiales

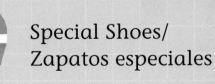

Roller Skates/
Patines con ruedas

Rico rolls on his board. Pop! Jump!

Rico rueda sobre su patineta.
¡Pop! ¡Salta!

"Watch my new skateboard trick,"
says Rico.

"Mira mi truco nuevo sobre
la patineta", dice Rico.

"Can I try?" asks Robot.
"Sure," says Rico. He gives the
skateboard to Robot.

"¿Puedo probar?" pregunta Robot.
"Seguro", dice Rico. Él le da la
patineta a Robot.

8

"Are you okay?" asks Rico.
"I'm sad," says Robot.

"¿Estás bien?" pregunta Rico.
"Estoy triste", dice Robot.

13

"Don't be sad," says Rico. "It takes time to learn a new trick."

"No estés triste", dice Rico. "Lleva tiempo aprender un truco nuevo."

14

"It does?" asks Robot. "Can I try
again?"
"Sure," says Rico.

"¿De veras?" pregunta Robot.
"¿Puedo probar de nuevo?"
"Seguro", dice Rico.

Robot stands on the skateboard.
"What do I do?" he asks.

Robot se para sobre la patineta.
"¿Qué hago?" pregunta.

16

"Roll," says Rico. "Now jump."

"Rueda", dice Rico. "Ahora salta".

Crash! Robot falls on the ground.

¡Crash! Robot se cae al piso.

"Are you okay?" asks Rico.
"I cannot do it," says Robot.

"¿Estás bien?" pregunta Rico.
"No puedo hacerlo", dice Robot.

"It takes time to learn a new trick,"
says Rico.

"Lleva tiempo aprender un truco
nuevo", dice Rico.

"I see," says Robot.
"Let's fix you. Then you can try again,"
says Rico.

"Ya veo", dice Robot.
"Vamos a arreglarte. Después puedes
tratar de nuevo".

Robot stands on the skateboard.
"Roll," says Rico.

Robot se para en la patineta.
"Rueda", dice Rico.

"Now what?" asks Robot.
"Jump on the rail," says Rico.

"¿Ahora qué?" pregunta Robot.
"Salta sobre la baranda", dice Rico.

Crack! The skateboard breaks in half.
"Oh, no!" says Rico.

¡Crack! La patineta se parte por la mitad.
"¡Oh, no!" dice Rico.

"Don't be sad," says Robot.
"I can make you a new one."

"No te pongas triste", dice Robot.
"Puedo hacerte una nueva".

"I can make two," says Robot.
"One for you and one for me."

"Puedo hacer dos", dice Robot.
"Una para ti y una para mí".

Robot gets to work.

Robot se pone a trabajar.

Robot gives Rico the new skateboard.
"Thanks!" says Rico.

Robot le da a Rico la patineta nueva.
"¡Gracias!" dice Rico.

"Now it is my turn," says Robot.
"Watch this trick."

"Ahora es mi turno", dice Robot.
"Mira este truco".

Zoom! Roll! Jump! Robot does a great new trick.

¡Zoom! ¡Rueda! ¡Salta! Robot hace un truco nuevo grandioso.

"You did it!" yells Rico.
"Let's do it again!" says Robot.

"¡Lo hiciste!" grita Rico.
"¡Hagámoslo de nuevo!" dice Robot.

story words

roll   skateboard

jump   trick

palabras del cuento

rodar   patineta

saltar   truco